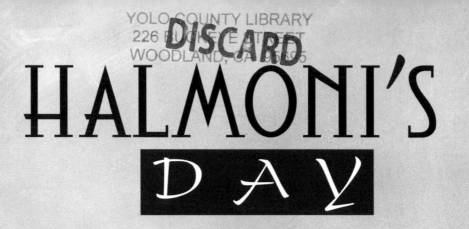

# HALMONI'S DAY

## EDNA COE BERCAW
### pictures by ROBERT HUNT

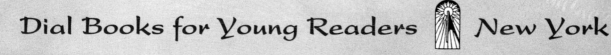

**Dial Books for Young Readers** ◈ **New York**

Published by Dial Books for Young Readers
A division of Penguin Putnam Inc.
345 Hudson Street
New York, New York 10014

Text copyright © 2000 by Edna Coe Bercaw
Pictures copyright © 2000 by Robert Hunt
All rights reserved
Designed by Julie Rauer
Printed in Hong Kong on acid-free paper
First Edition
1  3  5  7  9  10  8  6  4  2

Library of Congress Cataloging in Publication Data
Bercaw, Edna Coe.
Halmoni's day/by Edna Coe Bercaw; pictures by Robert Hunt.
p.  cm.
Summary: Jennifer, a Korean American, is worried that her grandmother,
visiting from Korea, will embarrass her on her school's Grandparents' Day,
but the event brings her understanding and acceptance.
ISBN 0-8037-2444-6
[1. Grandmothers—Fiction. 2. Korean Americans—Fiction. 3. Schools—Fiction.]
I. Hunt, Robert, date, ill. II. Title.
PZ7.B44814Hal  2000  [Fic]—dc21  98-47169  CIP  AC

The artwork was rendered in oils on paper.

## Glossary/Pronunciation Guide

NOTE: ALL SYLLABLES ARE STRESSED EQUALLY

✿

*halmoni* (hahl-mah-nee): grandmother

*ye-ppeu-da* (ee-puh-dah): to be pretty

*An-nyeong-ha-se-yo* (Ahn-nyong-ha-say-oh): This greeting can mean "Good morning,"
"Good afternoon," "Good evening," or even "How are you,"
depending on when it is given. Its literal meeting is "Are you at peace?"

✿

FOR MOM, WITH LOVE

*E.C.B.*

FOR NONA

*R.H.*

The silver gate finally swung open and a crowd of passengers eagerly pressed forward. Jennifer stood on tiptoe as she searched for Halmoni, her grandmother from Korea.

"Is that her?" she cried, pointing toward a tall, cheerful woman in a bright floral dress and matching hat.

"No, look, there she is!" her father exclaimed. Jennifer spun around to see a small woman in an elaborate silk gown approaching them. She chattered in Korean as Jennifer's mom wrapped her own mother in a huge hug.

Blinking hard, all Jennifer could think about was school the next day. Halmoni had arrived just in time for Grandparents' Day.

Jennifer wondered what her classmates would think of this tiny woman in strange clothes. Halmoni didn't even speak English!

"Aren't you going to welcome your grandmother?" Jennifer's mother whispered, gently nudging her forward.

"*An-nyeong-ha-se-yo,*" she stammered, struggling to remember the Korean greeting she had practiced over and over at home. Embarrassed, Jennifer lowered her eyes toward the shiny airport floor. She felt two thin arms wrap around her in a tight embrace. Looking up at Halmoni's joyful face, Jennifer smiled shyly. Then she bowed slowly and carefully.

Jennifer's parents each took one of Halmoni's bags. Then they walked Halmoni arm-in-arm through the bustling airport while Jennifer lagged a few steps behind. Glancing around, she noticed several other Korean ladies dressed like Halmoni. In school, she thought, everyone else's grandmother will be wearing American clothes.

"Jennifer *ye-ppeu-da,*" Halmoni was saying.

"What did she say?" Jennifer asked.

"She says you're pretty," her mother told her proudly. Jennifer began to feel a little better.

"There is a fourteen-hour time difference between here and Korea," Dad explained on the ride home.

"Halmoni may need to rest when we get back," Mom added, "because even though it's close to noontime here, it is still the middle of the night in Korea!"

"Wow," said Jennifer, wondering what it would be like to live in Halmoni's faraway country.

When they arrived home, Jennifer showed Halmoni to the guest room. Then she went downstairs into the kitchen.

"Mom, Dad, are you sure Halmoni should come to school tomorrow?" Jennifer asked. "Maybe she wants to just rest and relax here instead. I mean, Halmoni's got to be tired from her long flight and everything. . . ."

Jennifer's voice trailed off as Halmoni came into the kitchen. She picked up Jennifer's hand and gave it a warm squeeze. Jennifer gazed into the kind eyes twinkling with excitement. She gave her grandmother's hand a gentle squeeze back, wondering how Halmoni could understand so much when she did not speak English.

"I'm sure Halmoni is just fine, honey," Mom replied with a reassuring smile and a wink. As Jennifer helped set the table for brunch, her father suggested that she tell them all about the events planned at school the next day.

"Well, everyone made up special Grandparents' Day awards,"
Jennifer began, "and Mrs. Hillner asked that the grandparents be prepared
to share a favorite story or memory with the class."

As Dad translated for Halmoni, Jennifer leaned over and whispered in her grandmother's ear.

"But only if you want to, Halmoni. You don't have to say anything, if you don't want to."

Halmoni smiled warmly and answered back in Korean. "She says she'll have to think about what to say," Dad told Jennifer, "but I have a feeling that Halmoni will come up with something pretty special!"

At school the next day, everyone was busy finishing their Grandparents' Day projects and awards when Mrs. Hillner placed a brightly decorated box on her desk.

"If you are done with your award, please put it in this box," she told the class.

Jennifer had covered her envelope with drawings of daffodils and tulips. As she brought it up to Mrs. Hillner, she turned the envelope over, wondering if her award was such a good idea after all. Then her best friend, Martha, beckoned to her.

"Jennifer! Want to help me put up the family trees?"

"Sure!"

Jennifer tucked her envelope carefully into the box and hurried over to help her friend.

"I can't wait until everyone comes!" Martha exclaimed, handing Jennifer the masking tape. "I hope there's enough time to show them my science project!"

Jennifer quietly passed strips of masking tape to Martha, thinking again about how far away Halmoni lived. She was the only grandparent Jennifer had ever known, yet Jennifer could barely remember her last visit four years ago.

If only I knew her better, she wished.

After lunch Mrs. Hillner brought in more chairs. The children pushed their desks to one side to make room for everyone to sit down.

At exactly one-thirty, the grandparents began entering the room. Jennifer's face flushed when she saw her mother and grandmother enter. After everyone was seated, Mrs. Hillner greeted the crowded classroom.

"Welcome, grandparents and parents, and thank you all for coming. We have an exciting program planned for today! The children worked very hard on the wonderful family projects here on display. They even created their own Grandparents' Day awards for you. As we present the awards, we would love to hear any stories or memories you might want to share. Have fun, and remember, today is your day!"

Jennifer thought about those last words.

"Halmoni's day," she whispered to herself, and turned to look at her grandmother sitting quietly in her beautiful silk dress. Jennifer couldn't help but notice how different she was from the other grandparents, dressed in their running shoes and casual clothes. From across the room Halmoni caught Jennifer's stare and smiled at her. Jennifer smiled back and felt her heart begin to pound.

Lauren volunteered to pick the first envelope.

"This award is for the grandparent or grandparents who have the most grandchildren enrolled in the school!"

Christopher's grandparents collected that award and named all eleven of their grandchildren aloud. Next, Martha's grandparents recalled baby-sitting her for the first time. "We stood by Martha's crib for hours, just waiting to play with her, but instead, she slept all day."

The classroom filled with laughter and applause as the other grandparents received their awards and shared special family memories. There was an award for the youngest and then the oldest grandparent, and one for the grandparent who had served the longest in the military. There was even one for the best runner—Joshua's grandmother, who had just completed her sixth marathon!

Before long, Mrs. Hillner was reaching into the box for one final award.

"This award is for the grandparent who traveled the farthest to get here today."

That was Jennifer's award. All eyes turned toward Halmoni as Jennifer sank way down into her seat. Mom translated for Halmoni and together they stood to accept the award. "I'd like to introduce my mother from South Korea, Mrs. Lee," Mom said. "Jennifer calls her Halmoni." She explained that *"halmoni"* means "grandmother" in Korean.

Then Halmoni began to speak, her voice chiming softly as Jennifer's mom translated her words for the class.

"What I remember most when I was your age were the stories Mother would tell me about Father, an officer in the army who went away to fight in the Korean War. The war lasted for three years, and after it was over, we anxiously awaited Father's return. Instead, we did not hear from him for almost two more years."

She paused as a hush fell over the classroom.

"Mother had told me why he had to leave our peaceful village, and she promised he would return someday. I never doubted her words, but worried that he might not find us or remember me. I had forgotten so much about him as the years passed that I wondered if he would forget me too."

Halmoni's voice quivered but she continued her story.

"Just before I turned nine, I was working in the fields on an unusually hot day when I noticed a man approaching from the distance. I raced toward him as fast as I could. I ran and ran until I got close enough to see that it wasn't Father. It couldn't be. This man walked with a cane and was too gaunt, not at all like the proud man I wanted to remember. I backed away, my face red with embarrassment, and my heart felt like it would burst from the flood of tears I tried so hard to contain."

The school bell rang, and the sounds of racing footsteps in the hallway filled the classroom. But inside the class no one moved.

"As I turned away, the man began singing an old song that I instantly recognized. It brought forth memories of Father, ones I thought I had forgotten. Suddenly I could picture us chasing crickets after dark and laughing together. I knew at that moment that Father was home! I ran to him and we embraced. He held me so tight. I remember how safe I felt in his arms. I never wanted to let go."

Jennifer felt the tears that had been welling up in her eyes spill down her cheeks.

"The years we had spent apart made our time together so meaningful. But as the years passed, Father's constant coughing gradually took away his beautiful voice. We learned to communicate without words. The touch of a hand or a simple nod of the head conveyed so much. Father's expressive eyes were truly the windows to his heart and soul. Through them I could understand his thoughts, and feel his courage and kindness."

"Today I find that the greatest joy of being a grandparent is seeing parts of myself, my husband, and my parents live on through my children and their children. No one could remind me more of my own father than my American granddaughter, Jennifer!" Halmoni finished, her face radiant.

Jennifer jumped to her feet and made her way to the front of the classroom. Tears still falling, she kissed Halmoni warmly. "Today *is* your day, Halmoni," she whispered. "Thank you for making it mine too."